The Secret to Freedom

by Marcia Vaughan

illustrated by Larry Johnson

Lee & Low Books Inc.

New York

LEE & LOW BOOKS Inc., 95 Madison Avenue, New York, NY 10016
leeandlow.com

Manufactured in China by RR Donnelley Limited, October 2016

Book design by Tania Garcia
Book production by The Kids at Our House

The text is set in 14 pt. New Baskerville
The illustrations are rendered in acrylic

(HC) 15 14 13 12 11 10 9 8 7 6 5
(PB) 15 14 13 12 11 10 9 8
First Edition

Sources
Bial, Raymond. *The Underground Railroad.* Boston: Houghton Mifflin, 1995.
Haskins, Jim. *Get On Board: The Story of the Underground Railroad.* New York: Scholastic, 1993.
Hurmence, Belinda. *Slavery Time When I Was Chillun.* New York: Philomel, 1997.
Perdue, Charles L., Jr., Thomas E. Barden, and Robert K. Phillips, eds. *Weevils in the Wheat:*
    Interviews With Virginia Ex-Slaves. Charlottesville: University Press of Virginia, l976.
Tobin, Jacqueline L. and Raymond G. Dobard, Ph.D. *Hidden In Plain View: A Secret of Quilts*
    and the Underground Railroad. New York: Doubleday, 1998.

Library of Congress Cataloging-in-Publication Data
Vaughan, Marcia K.
        The secret to freedom / by Marcia Vaughan ; illustrated by Larry Johnson.— 1st ed.
            p.   cm.
        Summary: Great Aunt Lucy tells a story of her days as a slave, when she and her
brother, Albert, learned the quilt code to help direct other slaves and, eventually, Albert
himself, to freedom in the north.
        ISBN-13: 978-1-58430-021-2 (hardcover)   ISBN-13: 978-1-58430-251-3 (paperback)
        1. Underground railroad—Juvenile fiction. [1. Underground railroad—Fiction.
2. Slavery—Fiction. 3. Afro-Americans—Fiction. 4. Quilts—Fiction.] I. Johnson, Larry,
1949- ill. II. Title.
PZ7.V452 Sg 2001
[E]—dc21   00-064110

For Richard and Sam, who have brought laughter, love, and adventure into my life over and over again

— M.V.

We drink from wells that we didn't dig. We warm ourselves by fires that we didn't start. To every man, woman, or child who risked their lives for us to be free

— L.J.

I was ten years old the first time I went to stay with my Great Aunt Lucy. We'd shoo crows from the field, cool our feet in the river, then sit in the kitchen chitchatting like a pair of summer sparrows. I remember one day we were shelling peas into a chipped blue bowl while the curtains billowed in the breeze beside us.

Suddenly my gaze caught a splash of color on the wall.

"Aunt Lucy," I said. "Why do you keep that old scrap of cloth hanging over there?"

Aunt Lucy split open a pod and chased the peas out with her thumb.

"Child," she said, "that's a story I haven't told in a long, long time."

When I was about your age, I was a slave, property of folks named Briggs down in South Carolina. Seeing as I was born with a lame leg, the Overseer said I was no good for field work. So I got sent to scrub clothes out in the hot sun till my hands were raw and my back ached like an old plow mule's.

From where I worked I'd look out across the plantation trying to find Papa stooped over in the cotton fields. Sometimes I'd snatch a glance up at the Big House, where Mama was seamstress. Though I couldn't see my brother, Albert, I'd hear the clang-bang of his hammer as he worked at the blacksmith's anvil.

Times were full of trouble. War was coming, sure. Folks up north talking 'bout putting an end to slavery. Folks down south bound to keep it.

Long about that time the Overseer came to our quarters.

"Bessie, Thomas," he said. "Slave trader's takin' you to the auction block today."

"What about Albert and Lucy?" Papa asked.

"They stayin' here," the Overseer snapped. "Just you two gettin' sold off."

Saddest thing I ever saw was my parents bein' led off to that wagon. Knew I'd never see Mama's smile or hear Papa's laugh again. Master, he buy us, sell us, beat us, work us till we died.

Oh, how I wished things could be different.

Albert felt same as me, and he come up with a plan. Whenever he was loaned out to work at another plantation, he'd find out all he could 'bout the Underground Railroad.

One time he come home with a burlap sack slung over his shoulder.

"Lucy," he said, "I got the secret to freedom inside this sack. Blacksmith over at the Mobley Plantation gave it to me."

Albert's eyes danced as he emptied the sack on the table.

"What you got here, Albert," I said, "is a bunch of raggle-taggle old quilts."

Albert chuckled. "No, Lucy. These quilts are special. Blacksmith told me each one has a secret message stitched right into it. Slaves who understand these messages have a better chance of escaping to freedom up north."

"What kind of secret messages?" I asked.

"Messages that tell folks what to do. When they see the quilt with the monkey wrench pattern, it tells folks to collect the tools they'll need when they run away," Albert explained.

"When folks see the one called the wagon wheel, it tells them time's come to pack their belongings. This quilt with the bear's paw says to follow the bear tracks north through the mountains."

A wave of excitement washed over me. I was beginning to understand.

"Is this one important?" I asked, pointing to a quilt with tumbling blocks.

"It's the *most* important," Albert replied. "Tumbling blocks tell folks it's time to run."

Then Albert's eyes got real serious. "You want to help slaves escape, Lucy?" he asked.

"Course I do!" I said.

"When the time's right, I'll tell you to hang a certain quilt on the fence by the road," Albert said. "Be sure you hang out the right one. Folks' lives be depending on you."

"But what if Master Briggs sees it?"

"Master, Mistress, even the Overseer won't pay no mind to some old slave quilt," Albert said. "But slaves planning to escape will know what the messages mean."

"How'll they know?" I asked.

" 'Cause I'll tell 'em."

That brother of mine was wily as a fox and brave as a bull. Things worked out just like Albert said. When he told me, I'd hang the monkey wrench quilt on the fence. Later in the week I'd hang out the wagon wheel quilt. Few days after that, the bear's paw one. Then after I'd hang out the tumbling blocks quilt, Albert would steal away quiet as a cat during the night. He'd meet the runaways at the graveyard and lead them to a hiding place down by the river, where they'd begin their journey to freedom.

One night, I remember the moon was riding low in the sky. Patrollers caught Albert coming back late without a pass.

"Time to teach you a lesson, boy," they said. Those men tied Albert to a tree and lashed him, lashed him hard till blood ran red down his back.

After that the Overseer took a mean dislike to Albert. Whipped him raw for no reason. But those whippings couldn't beat the spirit out of my brother.

"Albert," I said one night as I rubbed grease into his wounds, "you got to run."

Albert shook his head. "I ain't running, Lucy. I won't leave you."

"You got to go, Albert. The Overseer just waiting for a chance to beat the life outta you."

Albert rose to his feet. "Then we'll both go," he said.

"You know I can't move no faster than a snail," I argued. "I go and the patrollers catch us, sure."

Albert's face was stubborn. "Then I'll carry you, Lucy. All the way to freedom."

"No, Albert. You got to go without me," I said. "War be coming soon. If the North wins, all slaves be free."

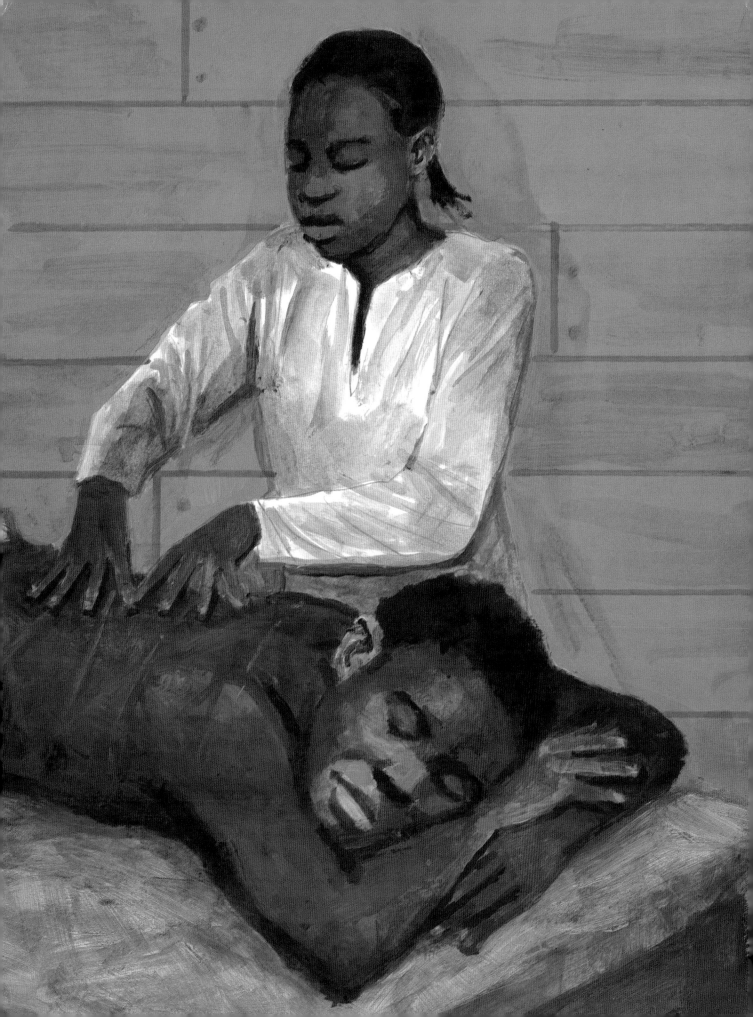

Albert held me in his arms and hugged me hard.

"Be a long time 'fore I see you again, Lucy," he whispered.

Tears hot as wash water flooded my eyes. I reached into my pocket.

"Take this with you, Albert," I said. "It's a quilt square I stitched with the North Star on it. It'll bring you luck."

Before I could say good-bye, he disappeared into the darkness.

In the distance thunder rumbled. Lightning flashed silver across the sky. I knew it was lighting the way for Albert. Then all was still.

Suddenly, the silence was shattered by the sound of Old Butler barking as he charged off into the night. There was the crack of gunfire and angry shouts.

Patrollers! Lord, I could barely breathe. I wanted to call out to Albert, but I couldn't. Couldn't do nothing 'cept clutch my quilt tight and pray to keep from screaming.

I had a horrible feeling I'd never see Albert again. Never knew if he got away that night or died trying. But my heart thundered like a drum to think maybe he was on his way to freedom.

War came. Slavery died a slow death. Life was still hard, but I knew I wanted to learn to read and write and teach others to do the same. Took a heap of time learning all those letters and how to string 'em into words.

I was all growed up by the time I started my own school in a brush arbor by the river. Didn't matter their age. Anybody wanted to learn, I'd teach 'em.

One specially hardworking pupil was a fellow named Chester. Every time he looked up at me, he'd get a grin wide as the Wateree River across his face.

A year later we got married. Chester worked as a sharecropper. I scrubbed clothes for a pittance and kept teaching for the love of it.

One afternoon the mailman came knocking at the door.
"Reckon this letter's been trying to find you for a long
time," he said, handing me a rumpled brown envelope.

Curious as a cat, I ripped it open. Out fell an old scrap
of fabric with a single star stitched on it.

"Heavens above, it's from Albert!" I cried. "He made it!"

After all those years I near burst with joy knowing my
brother was still alive.

"What's Albert got to say?" Chester asked.

My eyes raced across the paper. "He's living up in Port Hope, Canada. Says if this letter ever finds me, he wants to bring his family to visit. Oh Chester, I'm going to see my Albert. I'm going to hold him in my arms and hug him hard."

Oh my, did we ever have a celebration when Albert and his family came to town. In all my years that's the happiest thing ever happened to me.

Great Aunt Lucy smiled as she took that old quilt square off the wall and held it in her hands. Then she carried it to the table and let me hold it too.

"Now I do declare, child, your eyes sparkle just like Albert's did all those years ago," she said.

Then we sat in happy silence, shelling peas into the bowl while the curtains billowed in the breeze beside us.